BATTER UP
WOMBAT

HELEN LESTER
Illustrated by LYNN MUNSINGER

Houghton Mifflin Company Boston

Walter Lorraine *wn* Books

To Kate, the most beautiful
granddaughter in the history of the world.
And then some.

—H.L.

Walter Lorraine *wℓ* Books

Text copyright © 2006 by Helen Lester
Illustrations copyright © 2006 by Lynn Munsinger

www.houghtonmifflinbooks.com

Library of Congress Cataloging-in-Publication Data

Lester, Helen.
  Batter up Wombat / Helen Lester ; illustrated by Lynn Munsinger.
      p. cm.
  "Walter Lorraine books."
  Summary: An Australian wombat joins the Champs baseball team,
and even though he is disastrously ignorant about the game, his innate
talents save everyone when a tornado suddenly strikes.
  RNF ISBN-13: 978-0-618-73784-0   PA ISBN-13: 978-0-547-01549-1
  RNF ISBN-10: 0-618-73784-7   PA ISBN-10: 0-547-01549-6
  [1. Wombats—Fiction. 2. Animals—Fiction. 3. Baseball—Fiction.
4. Tornadoes—Fiction.] I. Munsinger, Lynn, ill. II. Title.
  PZ7.L56285Ba 2006
  [E]—dc22
                                                        2006004563

Printed in the Singapore
TWP   10 9 8 7 6 5 4 3 2

BATTER UP
WOMBAT

The Champs weren't.
Last year they finished last in the North American
Wildlife League.

LEAGUE STANDINGS
1. GIANTS
2. BEARS
3. SOX
4. BANDITS
5. KITTENS
6. YEARLINGS
7. CHAMPS

But this was a brand-new season, and they were ready to
go in their spiffy clean uniforms.

On the morning of the opening game they had been practicing their most athletic moves when suddenly, out of the blue, an outsider wandered onto the field.

"Who are you, big fella?" they inquired.
"I am a Wombat," replied the stranger.

"Whambat? Whambat!" The Champs jumped up and down in delight.
Wham! Bat! A big hitter! Just what their team needed!

The Wombat couldn't understand the source of their
excitement. And these folks sure talked funny.
Imagine calling a Wombat a Whambat.

But when they asked him to join their team, he was
as pleased as punch.

He loved games, and back in his faraway home of
Australia he had been quite a star at rugby.
"So, mates," asked the Wombat, "what's your game?"
"Baseball," came the reply.
"Oh. Baseball," said the Wombat. "Never heard of it."

The Champs realized that this promising newcomer would
need a quick course in the sport, so they sat him down
and gave him tips as fast as they could think of them.
"For starters, you'll need a bat.
The batboy takes care of bats."

"The pitcher stands on
a mound." *Mound of what?*
The Wombat blinked a few
times, shook his befuddled
head, and kept listening.

"Never stand on home plate."
Of course not,
thought the Wombat.
*Never stand on any plate.
Period. It's not
sanitary.*

His teammates continued,
"The catcher wears a mask
for his own protection.

Oh, and sometimes the
hitter hits a foul."
*Rough game, this
baseball,* thought
the Wombat.

He was growing more confused by the minute, but since
he was eager to play he stood up and announced, "All right,
mates, suit me up." Sure enough, in no time he looked
like a Champ.

His pleased teammates urged, "Now off for some practice in the batter's cage."

Cage? CAGE?

Not long after, there arrived a busload of raccoons.
This rival team bore the scary name "the Masked Bandits."
"What is THAT?" they asked, looking at the huge Wombat.
"Oh, it's only a Whambat," answered the Champs.

"Not fair," argued the Bandits. "We want that big thing on *our* team."

"Sorry," replied the Champs, as they counted the Bandits. "We need him to make the numbers even. No even numbers, no game." The Masked Bandits knew that rules were rules, and they grumbled their way to the field.

"Play ball!" called the umpire, and the game was under
way. The Champs were at bat.

"Batter up, Whambat," whispered his teammates. "You're
the next hitter."

The Wombat was alarmed. He really didn't care for hitting.

They shoved a hunk of wood into his paws, and WHAM!
As he raised the hunk of wood to protect himself from
the speeding ball, somehow it connected and the ball sailed into
the outfield. "Run!" yelled the Champs.

The Wombat ran, following
the signs to first,
and skidded into
second.

Moments later he heard,
"Steal third!
Steal third base!"
The Wombat stole third
base, but he didn't
know quite where
to hide it.

He hadn't much time to ponder, though, for his teammates called to him again, "Run home!" *Run home? All the way to Australia?* Now, that was asking a lot.

He needed to describe the length of such a journey to these mates, so instead of running he walked over to the Champs' bench to explain.

The umpire declared, "The outsider's out because he's outside the lines. Shucks, he's even off the field."

BALL 3			STRIKE 2				OUT 2			
	1	2	3	4	5	6	7	8	9	TOTAL
MASKED BANDITS	10	2	4	11	8	1	9			
CHAMPS	0	0	0	0	0	0	0			

And that was only the top of the first inning.
As the game progressed, things went from bad to worse
and the score grew in favor of the Masked Bandits.
The Champs desperately tried to coach their Whambat.

"Catch the fly!"
He caught two flies
and a duck.

"Get under the pop-up!"
Pop up?
What an odd request.

"Tag second!"
He tagged the
second baseman.
"You're it."

By now the Masked Bandits were giving high-fives and
celebrating the fact that the stranger was on the
other team, not theirs.

For his part, the Wombat was frazzled, exhausted, and very sad. He could hardly bear to look at the disappointed faces of his teammates, and he felt so . . . outside.

It was as though a big cloud was gathering over his head.

Actually, it was.

And over everybody else's head.
The sky grew dark. And they saw it.
"TORNADO!" shrieked the Champs, the Bandits, the umpire,
and the fans. "TO THE DUGOUT! TO THE DUGOUT!"

There was only one problem. There was no dugout.

After all, this wasn't major league baseball.

Dugout. Aha! Digging was the Wombat's specialty, for wombats were known to be capable of digging tunnels up to 655 feet long. Wasting no time, he began to dig a tunnel.

Into the tunnel raced the Champs, the Bandits, and the
umpire as the tornado sped closer. But there was no room
for the fans.
"Enlarge the tunnel!" everyone cried. "Make room for the fans!"
"Fans?" wondered the Wombat. "Capital idea. It's getting
quite stuffy in here."

Lying on his side in true Wombat form, he
duganddduganddduganddug,
enlarging the room further, and—
just in time—in rushed the fans. Huddled together, the
crowd trembled as the tornado whizzed and whirled
directly above them.

Then all was silent.
They were safe.
Inside.
And the most important insider was the outsider.

The Wombat may not have been a Whambat, but he was truly a Champ.

As for the rest of the game—
what do you think?